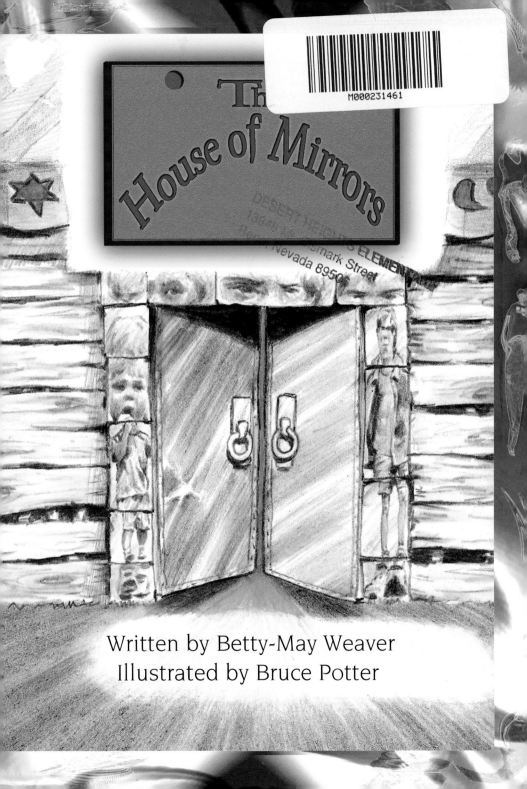

The House of Mirrors

Written by Betty-May Weaver
Illustrated by Bruce Potter

Katina and Laura loved the fair. Every year they were among the first to get tickets. They went on all the rides they could, but most of all they liked the scary things.

A large sign flashed "House of Mirrors" in bright red letters. You could see it from right across the fairground. As soon as they saw the sign, Katina and Laura ran to the ticket booth.

"I'll wait outside for you," said their older brother. "I'll be right here by the hot dog stand."

A small man with a funny little green top hat barked out, "Come on in to the House of Mirrors. You'll laugh so hard it'll make you cry."

There was something weird about the man. His eyes seemed to glow like two big fireflies and his ears pointed up outside his funny little green top hat, just like rabbits' ears.

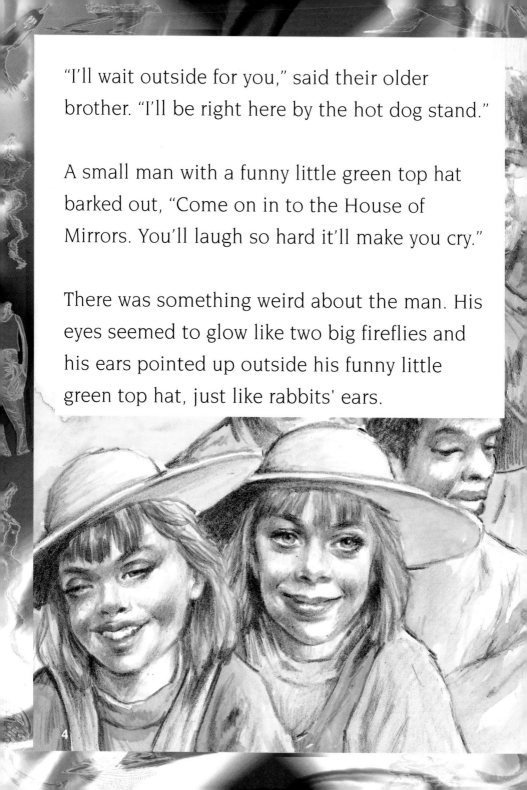

But Katina and Laura didn't care. They were too busy getting their money out of their pockets.

"Let's go," said Katina, "I want to see what you look like as a cone head."

The strange man took their money. Then he said with an odd sort of smile, "You're about to have the experience of a lifetime."

"You're weird," the girls shouted as they went into the House of Mirrors.

Inside was a short, narrow hall. It led to other halls, each with large curvy mirrors. Katina and Laura laughed and laughed as they looked into each mirror. They were short and fat, then tall and skinny. Sometimes their heads looked wide. Sometimes their heads looked pointed.

They laughed and laughed so hard it hurt. After laughing at each other for awhile, Katina and Laura walked outside again and went to find their brother at the hot dog stand.

As soon as they started walking, they knew something was wrong.

People stared at them and began to laugh. Their big brother laughed, too. Laura and Katina looked at each other and screamed.

"Oh no!" yelled Laura. "What's happened to you? You look just like you did in the last mirror!"

"So do you!" screamed Katina.

They couldn't believe it. Laura looked very strange. Her face was narrow, her legs were very long and her body was wide. Katina was just the opposite. Her legs were very short, her body was long and her head was wide.

But this time it wasn't so funny. They didn't want to look like this forever.

"What do we do now?" cried Katina.

"We have to do something fast," replied Laura.

"Go back to the man at the House of Mirrors," said their big brother. "Go back and ask that weird man what's happened."

They ran back to see the weird man at the ticket booth. He looked at them and began to laugh.

"Now who's weird?" asked the man.

"Your mirrors tricked us," the girls said.

"Oh I know," said the man.

"Well if you know, then you'll know how to turn us back to the way we were before we went into your stupid House of Mirrors," said Laura.

The funny man in the little green hat told them he did know how to change them back.

"If you want to know the secret, you'll have to pay me 10 times more than you paid to go in," he said.

"What a rip-off," said Katina. "But we can't stay looking like this."

So they gave the man the money he wanted and asked him to tell them the secret.

"Go into the House of Mirrors through the exit and walk through the halls backward," he said. "You'll see. It will undo everything. Then you'll look just like you used to again."

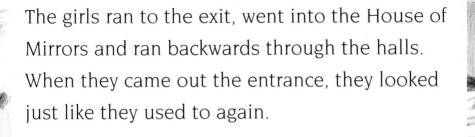

The girls ran to the exit, went into the House of Mirrors and ran backwards through the halls. When they came out the entrance, they looked just like they used to again.

"I said you'd have the experience of your lives," said the weird man with the little green hat and pointed ears.

Laura said, "He was right. It was an experience."

"Yeah," said Katina. "But it's an experience we could have done without. It was very, very scary. What if we couldn't change back?"

"Don't even think about it," said Laura. "Now what scary thing will we go on next?"